THERE'S MORE TO A BANANA

There's More to a Banana

Written by
RITA PHILLIPS MITCHELL

Illustrated by
PAUL HOWARD

WALKER BOOKS
AND SUBSIDIARIES

LONDON • BOSTON • SYDNEY

To Olga, Tessie, Sylvia and Gloria

First published 1999 by Walker Books Ltd
87 Vauxhall Walk, London SE11 5HJ

2 4 6 8 10 9 7 5 3 1

Text © 1999 Rita Phillips Mitchell
Illustrations ©1999 Paul Howard

This book has been typeset in Plantin Light.

Printed in England by Clays Ltd, St Ives plc

British Library Cataloguing in Publication Data
A catalogue record for this book
is available from the British Library.

ISBN 0-7445-5935-9

CONTENTS

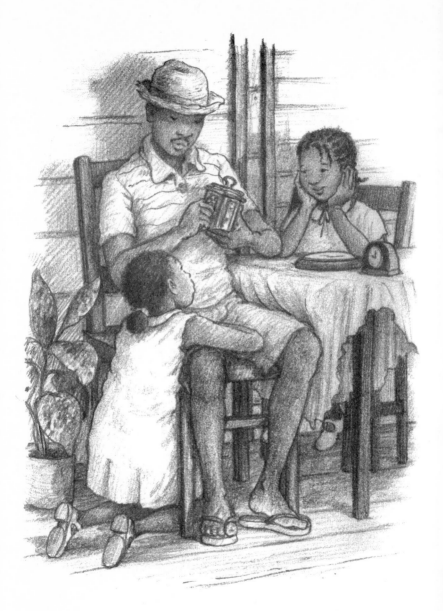

Sometimes he let Flora and me help him.

In a World Full of Clocks

Every Sunday after lunch my mother rested in her hammock. My father sat at a table beside her, cleaning and winding up all the clocks in our house and our gran's. Sometimes he let Flora and me help him. We handed him the tools and he showed us how to set the hands of the clocks at the right time. And every Sunday he would say, "In a world full of clocks there's no excuse for forgetting the time."

One Sunday when we had finished and the clocks were tick-tocking noisily away, my father decided to lie down in his hammock.

"Can we go to the park, Poppa?" I asked. My father nodded.

"Yes, but remember your gran expects her clocks today. See you get back here by four, no later."

"Yes, Poppa," we chorused. I put some marbles in my pocket and we dashed off. On the way to the park we pretended to be Poppa, saying out loud in a deep voice: "In a world full of clocks there's no excuse for forgetting the time."

When we got there, Dave Dee and Mitsy were playing marbles. Their friends crowded round.

"Who's winning?" I asked. Nobody said a word. "I want to play too."

"SSSSSHhh!" hissed the others.

Mitsy played well but in the end she lost three of her best marbles to Dave Dee. Dave

8

Dee was smug. He held up his bag full of marbles to the crowd.

"Who's next?" he said with a huge grin.

"I'll play," I cried.

"You're in a hurry to lose your marbles," scoffed Dave Dee.

"Who's losing?" I said.

"You have to wait your turn," said Dave Dee's best friend, Buck, "'cause I'm next." Buck blew on his marbles for luck. Then he examined each one before carefully setting them down on the ground.

I sighed. I could see that the game was going to take a long time. And they did play on and on. But just when I was thinking that I would never get my turn, Dave Dee won – yet again.

"You still going to play him?" said Mitsy.

"I said so, didn't I?"

"Oh, Mel!" whispered Flora. "You're going

to lose all your best marbles."

I dug down deep in my pocket. My marbles clinked. Suddenly I didn't think it was such a good idea either. But I couldn't back down now. I held three marbles in my hand.

Win! Win! Win! I said inside my head.

"What are you waiting for, Mel?" Dave Dee called out. "Meow! Meow! Oh, my! You're a scaredy-cat." Dave's friends began to snigger. It made me angry.

"I'm no scaredy-cat," I said, putting the marbles down as targets. "You go first."

Once we started playing everything else went out of my head. I concentrated hard. The only sound I heard was the CLINK-CLINK of marble against marble and the ooohs and aaahs of the crowd. We played six games and Dave Dee and me were level-

The only sound I heard was the CLINK-CLINK
of marble against marble.

pegging. Dave Dee wasn't laughing any more.

"Girl, you can play for sure!" said Mitsy.

"It's a fluke," said Dave Dee's friends.

"Winner takes all on the next game," said Dave Dee, trying to sound confident.

It was my turn to go first. I crouched down. I lined up my shot. I got my eye straight on Dave Dee's huge, sparkling green marble. Everybody sucked in their breath at the same time. At that very moment the park clock struck a mighty DONG!

"Oh, no!" I cried, grabbing up my marbles. "Come on, Flora, we've got to go!"

"You can't run away now," cried Dave Dee. "It's not fair." Everyone was shouting at me.

"I must go," I said.

"Is it four o'clock already?" asked Flora.

"You're kidding – it's five o'clock!" someone said.

We tore out of the park like two wild things. We reached the top of our street in quick time. But Poppa was there before us. His hair was standing straight up on his head like the fur of an angry cat.

"Uh-oh!" said Flora, dropping a step behind me.

"HELLO! So you *do* know you have a home to come to," said Poppa, smiling an alligator kind of smile.

Stay cool, I told myself.

Flora lagged even further behind and the gap between us got bigger and bigger. Without saying another word my father turned and walked off. I knew I had to follow him ... through the gate, up the stairs and into the kitchen. I glanced round. Flora was far behind me.

"What time is it?" Poppa said, pointing to the kitchen clock.

My heart went bop. The clock ticked.

"Ten minutes past five?" I said in a thin voice.

"So you *do* know how to tell the time," said my father.

"Oh, yes," Flora cried from the doorway. "Melanie can tell the time real good and I can and all."

"Is that soooo?" my father said. "How come you are late then?"

"I was playing marbles, Poppa, and…"

My father winced as if he had been bitten by a mosquito.

"Marbles! Playing! That's no excuse for forgetting the time!" he said. "There's a clock in the park, isn't there?"

"Y-yes," we said reluctantly.

"Sorry, Poppa," I added. "Next time we'll

keep looking at the clock."

"See that you do," my father said, shooing us away. "Though I still have to consider whether there'll be a next time or not."

"I wish clocks hadn't been invented," I said as we got ready to go to Grandma's. "They make life so boring!"

"It's so hard to remember to look at them when you're having a good time," agreed Flora. "I bet grown-ups sometimes forget too."

"They sure talk as if they don't," I said.

The next day my mother went to visit a friend. My father was sitting on the stairs where it was cool.

"I've just put the cassava cake in the oven," my mother told him as she was leaving. "It should be ready by three-thirty. Make sure

15

you take it out. Don't forget, now."

"Forget! Me? You know me and good timekeeping," said my father, pretending to be offended.

"Just remember," said my mother. "Unless, of course, you don't want cassava cake for supper."

"Stop worrying, Momma," said my father, checking his watch.

Later, my friend Murve and I were doing roll-overs in the sandpit. Flora tried to copy us but she kept falling sideways.

"Tuck your head well down between your knees," my father called. "That way your shoulders and not your neck will take your weight."

It wasn't long before Flora was shouting at the top of her voice, "Look, everybody! I can do it!"

"I didn't know you were into gymnastics," Murve said to my father.

"Sure do," he said, flexing his muscles. "I was a champion gymnast in my teens and could have turned professional."

"No kidding!" said Murve.

"No kidding," my father said. "Here, I'll show you."

He bent down, clasping his ankles. His bones crackled. He tucked his head between his knees. His bones crackled some more. Then he did a slow roll-over. When he straightened up he was smiling broadly.

"Not bad, eh?" he said.

"Now that's a laughable sight," said Murve's dad, looking over the fence. "Don't you think you're past it, old boy?"

"Look who's talking!" said my father. "You can't even touch your toes."

My father and Murve's dad were great

friends, but that never stopped them having a go at each other every chance they got.

"I wasn't always like this you know," said Murve's dad, patting his stomach. "I was the amateur champion gymnast of my home town. I was even going to turn professional."

"Ha! Ha! Ha!" My father threw his head back. "Don't make me laugh!"

Murve's dad didn't seem to like that. He came running into our yard.

"Come on, then," he said, "let's see who's the real champion here."

"If you're not afraid to make a spectacle of yourself, I'm game," said my father, doing a cartwheel. Murve's dad did a cartwheel too. Then they both stood there puffing and blowing.

"Poppa! Poppa! Move out of the way please," I said. "We want a go!"

"Wait a minute," Poppa said between

*"If you're not afraid to make a spectacle of yourself,
I'm game," said my father, doing a cartwheel.*

great puffs of breath. "We'll take turns doing cartwheels and the one who lasts the longest will be the winner."

"You're on," said Murve's dad.

"Yeeeeaaah!" we shouted.

"They'll soon get tired out," Murve whispered.

Murve's dad went first and we counted each cartwheel loudly. We had got to seven when he stopped suddenly. He just flopped down on his back and stayed there with his arms and legs spread out on the grass. His chest was pumping up and down.

Then it was my father's turn. We counted to nine before he gave up. He went over to Murve's dad.

"Call yourself a champion!" he said, giving him a hand to help him up.

They held on to each other, laughing and

panting, their T-shirts wringing wet. They were making so much noise we didn't notice Momma had come back.

"Shame on you two," she called. "You're worse than the children."

After Murve and his dad had gone, my mother turned to us, "Hurry up and wash your hands, girls. Supper will be ready in two ticks."

As soon as my mother mentioned supper, the veins popped up fat on my father's forehead.

"Caramba!" he groaned and fled up the stairs.

"You never! You couldn't have!" cried my mother, running up behind him.

When Flora and I got to the kitchen the oven door was open and there was smoke everywhere. My mother was staring at the baking dish. The cassava cake had turned into a piece of smoking charcoal. My father chased the smoke out of the kitchen. Then he just stood there shifting from one foot to the other. Flora and I kept as quiet as we could.

Finally my father said, "Come on, girls, we'll cook supper tonight."

"And that will make everything all right, I suppose," said my mother sharply.

"I'm sorry, dear," said Poppa. "I clean forgot."

"Forgot!" snapped my mother. "The man who knows all about good timekeeping forgot the time! Don't you dare go on about clocks ever again."

Flora and I looked at each other the way you do when you find out something for the very first time. Then Flora sidled up to me and whispered, "You see, Mel, Poppa forgot what he told us not to forget. Hee-hee-hee!"

"Now you know," I whispered back, "grown-ups can forget too – even in a world full of clocks!"

*I put my hands over my ears and walked
away from her.*

A PROPER LITTLE NURSE

It was Wednesday. I was excited. My friend Murve's birthday was coming up soon. My mother had promised to take me out on Saturday and buy me a new dress for the party. It was blue and beautiful with shiny studs all over. I talked about that dress so much Flora got fed up with me.

"I bet somebody else will buy it before Saturday," said Flora.

"Shut up, Flora," I cried. "I'm not listening." I put my hands over my ears and walked away from her. I was actually thinking the same thing but I couldn't bear hearing it said out loud. By Friday I was so excited that I couldn't stop talking.

"Shopping tomorrow," I kept saying to Flora. It was her turn to put both hands over her ears. But that didn't stop me. As we got into bed that night I said, "I bet you wish you were getting a new dress. Oh, happy, happy me!" Flora hissed like a snake and turned her back to me.

The next morning when I opened my eyes it was later than usual.

"Melanie! Hurry up!" shouted my mother from the kitchen. "Breakfast is ready."

I had expected to feel even more excited than the day before. Instead, I felt uncomfortable. When I swallowed my throat hurt. When I got up I felt dizzy.

"What's the matter with me?" I mumbled to myself.

I flopped down at the breakfast table.

26

Even the smell of freshly baked bread didn't perk me up. I didn't want to talk and Flora's constant yapping hurt my head.

"Eat up and be quick about it, Melanie," said my mother, her head in the fridge. "I want to make an early start."

"This bread is hot and lovely," said Flora. I just sat there holding my head.

"What's come over you, Melanie?" said my mother, sitting down. "All week you were full of beans. Where have all the beans gone today?"

Flora giggled. "She planted them in the yard," she said. "And maybe she's forgotten that today is Saturday and it's supposed to be her happy-happy day."

"I'm not feeling well," I cried irritably. My mother looked at me. She put down the bread knife and ran her hand over my forehead.

"You seem to have a slight temperature,"

she said. "Get some food inside you; it'll keep your strength up."

"I can't, Momma," I said, giving her a pleading look. "My throat's too sore."

"Then drink this," she said, pouring warm milk into my cup. "It'll make you feel better."

Minutes after drinking the milk, I felt sick. My mother rushed me to the bathroom. Afterwards she told me to lie down on the sofa and gave me some white stuff to drink.

"This will settle your stomach," she reassured me. I made a face and held my throat.

"Yuck!" said Flora when my mother left the room. "Nasty stuff."

"Shut up, Flora," I said. "You're lucky, you don't have to take any medicine."

"Luck has nothing to do with it. I'm

stronger than you, that's all," said Flora. "You catch everything that's going and I don't – even Momma says so."

"You're right for once, Flora," I said. "You never catch anything, not even your breath."

"Fun-ny! Fun-ny!" said Flora. "It'll serve you right if somebody else buys that dress."

Just then my father came into the room.

"Don't worry, Momma," he called. "Melanie's OK. She and Flora are back to normal, arguing."

My mother came back in. "Are you really feeling better, Melanie?" she asked.

"I think so," I said. "But what about the dress, Momma?"

"You're going nowhere today, my girl. You must rest," said my mother. "That dress will still be there when you're better."

"And if you don't get better in time for Murve's party then Momma can buy a dress for me instead," said Flora.

"Wish, wish!" I said.

Then suddenly I began to feel ill again. My eyes watered. I felt sticky. My inside was on fire. My outside was on fire.

"Help!" I shouted. But it sounded far away.

The next time I opened my eyes, Momma, Poppa and Flora were by my bed.

"What happened?" I said through cracked lips.

"We know you love to sleep but you broke the record this time, my girl," said my mother, smiling. "You slept and slept, right round the clock."

"Yes," said Flora. "And the doctor came and you didn't know a thing."

"How's my sleeping beauty?" asked my father cheerfully. "Feeling better?"

I nodded and tried to smile.

*The next time I opened my eyes, Momma, Poppa
and Flora were by my bed.*

"Sleeping beauty? No way!" said Flora. "*She* slept for a hundred years, remember."

"All right, Flora," said my father.

"The doctor says you've caught a tummy bug," my mother told me. "There are a few other children with the same problem – all you have to do now is eat and you'll get better." While she went to get me some food, my father and Flora kept on talking, sometimes to me, sometimes to each other. My eyelids started to get heavier and heavier as the voices droned on and on in my head. I fell asleep.

When I woke up again, my mother brought me some soup. But my lips were so cracked they hurt, and I found it hard to swallow.

"You have to eat something, Melanie," she kept telling me. She tried to get me to eat all that day but I kept pushing the food away.

The next day she tried again. She fussed and coaxed and eventually got upset and told me off.

"Nobody can live without food," she said as she went out of the room. "If you don't eat you're going to die."

Just then Flora came to the door. Hearing my mother's words she gasped and covered her mouth with her hand.

"You shouldn't be listening at the keyhole, Flora," said my mother in her crossest voice.

"I didn't mean to, Momma, honest," said Flora. "I was just coming to see Melanie."

"I believe you, Flora," said my mother after a few seconds. "I'm sorry."

That afternoon Flora came into my room with a steaming tamale. It's our absolutely favourite dish and Momma only cooks it on special occasions. It's made from maize flour and pork with lots of spices, wrapped in a plantain leaf and steamed.

"Look what I have," said Flora. "It's lovely and I helped Momma to make it. Can you smell it, Mel?"

"Take it away. I don't want anything," I said.

"Don't be silly. You've never refused a tamale in your life," said Flora.

"Well, it never smelled so awful before."

"That's because when you're ill you smell things upside down," said Flora.

"I don't want..." I began. But before I could finish what I was saying, Flora spooned a piece of tamale into my mouth.

"Chew," she said sharply, holding her hand in front of my mouth to stop me spitting anything out.

I stared at Flora dumbfounded. I could hardly believe what she was doing.

"Chew, Melanie," she repeated. "You must eat. You have to."

I closed my eyes and started to move my jaws very slowly. But Flora wasn't taking any chances. She refused to take her hand away from my lips until I swallowed. I swallowed. She took away her hand and made herself more comfortable on the bed. Pleased with her success, Flora got bolder and cheekier.

"From now on I'm going to look after you and make sure you eat up your food," she told me.

"You don't have to do that, Flora," I said.

"But I want you to get better. It's boring without you and I don't have anyone to play with," Flora said. "Besides, you've got to get better so you can go to Murve's birthday party."

Flora was talking like she was a grown-up. I looked at her. I mean *really* looked. And I

35

noticed something else. She was behaving as if she cared, not like my little sister at all. But just as I started to relax, she tickled me.

"Aaaaaah!" I cried out. CLICK! The spoon hit my teeth. "Noooo! Stop!"

Flora paid me no mind whatsoever. She pushed another piece of tamale in my mouth and demanded that I chew it.

"I'm not leaving you alone until I think you have eaten enough," she told me firmly.

I figured if I ate the next spoonful without fussing she might give me a break. Then I looked up and saw Momma at the door. I don't know how long she'd been watching us.

"Oh, Flora!" she cried. "You've done it; you've got Melanie to eat!" Then my mother hugged Flora and kissed her and Flora's grin spread from ear to ear. And then they both hugged me.

*Then my mother hugged Flora and kissed her and
Flora's grin spread from ear to ear.*

From then on, Flora put herself in charge of meals. She wouldn't leave me alone until she was satisfied I'd eaten enough. I called her a bossyboots but deep down I knew she was the best sister ever.

When I got better, I had lots of visitors. My grandmother and Uncle Bill were the first, then the neighbours. But mostly the house was full of Flora's friends. They wanted to know every detail of how she got me to eat when even my mother couldn't. And Flora was more than happy to tell them, over and over again. I was a bit embarrassed. But I was proud of her, too.

One evening we sat in the front room.

"Come on, Flora," said Poppa, looking straight at her with narrowed eyes and a smile. "What made you such a good little nurse?"

"Melanie wasn't eating anything and I thought she was going to die," said Flora.

"Why did you think that?" asked my father.

"I heard Momma say so," said Flora in a tiny voice.

"Well, Momma and I think that it was something else – we think it was because you love Melanie and that's why you're turning out to be such a good little sister. How about that?"

Flora didn't know what to say. She started to look at her wriggling toes. After a few seconds she glanced at me, then at Momma and finally at Poppa.

"Weeell?" said Poppa, raising an eyebrow.

"I suppose so," said Flora at last.

I gave her a hug and soon we were giggling together.

"*I suppose so* seems to be the best answer we are going to get right now," Poppa told Momma.

"I suppose so, too," said Momma, and they burst out laughing.

After we stopped laughing, Momma handed me a shopping bag.

"I can still go to Murve's party!" I shouted with delight as I took out the blue dress.

"Well now," said Poppa, handing Flora a present. "I think the little nurse in our family deserves something too. Right, Momma?"

"Sure do," said Momma.

"Thank you," said Flora, and immediately started to tear the wrapper off.

A few minutes later she was strutting around the room in a new nurse's uniform.

"You look like a proper little nurse now," we told her.

The sun streaked through the brims of our hats.

Busman's Holiday

The day after school broke up we set off on our holidays to Bright Springs. Momma helped Flora and me get dressed. We put on new shorts and tops with pictures of trees and birds printed all over. Then Momma pulled our straw hats down, right over our foreheads.

"That will keep the glare out of your eyes," she said, squinting up at the bright sky. But the sun still streaked through the brims of our hats. We began turning our heads from side to side, making lacy patterns jump about on our faces.

In quick time Poppa got his truck ready.

"Melanie! Flora! Hop in!" he cried, getting behind the wheel. We climbed in. Momma sat beside us and we drove out of our yard.

"We're off," said Momma. "At last!"

"We're off on our summer holidays, Poppa, Momma, Melanie and me," chanted Flora.

"Actually, *I* am off on a—" said Poppa in a voice as low as the engine. Then he paused. He raised one bushy eyebrow, which made the other eye crunch up small. I could tell he was about to come up with something tricky. "—busman's holiday."

"What kind of holiday is that?" Flora and I said together.

"I'll be driving on a farm," said Poppa. "I figure the money will come in handy."

"What's a bus doing on a farm?" asked Flora, puzzled.

We all laughed. But actually, I didn't understand either until Poppa explained.

"I'll be driving my truck," he said. "And since I also drive my truck in my regular job, that's called a busman's holiday."

"Then a busman's holiday isn't a holiday at all," I said.

"Why can't you have a holiday-holiday?" moaned Flora.

"Quiet now, girls. Let your poor father concentrate," said Momma as Poppa turned into a wide road.

"This is the Northern Highway," said Poppa. "It leads straight to Mexico."

"Mexico!" we shouted. "Can we go there?"

"*No hoy*," said Poppa. "*Otra vez*."

We wrinkled up our faces.

Poppa said, "That's Spanish for 'Not today, another time'."

Poppa drove on and on. The road was straight, with the Old River on one side and farms on the other. We saw cattle chewing and chewing. They seemed to be always eating, yet they looked so skinny. Flora and I tried counting their ribs but we were going too fast. We passed little houses with shady porches and barking dogs. We passed other travellers. Sometimes they waved to us and we waved back. Suddenly Momma pointed to a huge tamarind tree. "Turn right here," she said.

The road turned into a dirt track and dropped down into a gully. Flora and I caught our breath.

"I'm scaaared!" Flora cried out.

"Me too!" I said.

Then the truck climbed slowly up and out of the gully. There were rocks and clumps of hard earth everywhere. The truck started bumping and rattling, and the words kept bouncing out of our mouths.

"Hold on toooo youuuur seeeeeeatsss!" said Poppa.

Flora and I laughed. We liked the way the words jumped and stretched like elastic in the air. As we bumped higher and higher we shouted out, "Mouuntain Piiiiine Ridge! Maaaahoganeeeeeeeee! Wiiiiiigle waaaaaagle booooooaaaaaa constrictor!"

"Eeeee-nnnnnufff!" my mother spluttered.

Not long after, my father pulled up sharply in front of a little wooden cottage with a thatched roof. My mother took a bottle of lemonade out of the back of the truck and we gulped it down.

"Perfect," she said, looking around. "Certainly worth all that hill and gully ride."

"Sure piece of heaven this is!" Poppa told her, sniffing the air. "Just like when I was a

47

boy." He sniffed again. "Lemons, guavas, the river and freshly baked earth smells all mixed up together. I tell you man, this is a natural perfume factory!"

The cottage was by itself on high ground. All around it were tall trees. Flora and I picked out a few houses between the trees. They seemed far away. A big barn with a yellow roof was the closest.

"What's that?" I said.

"That's the grocery shop, hardware store and post office all rolled into one," said Poppa.

"I can't see any other children," said Flora in a moany voice. "What kind of place is this? It's all jungly and lonely."

"Ha!" said Poppa. "I reckon it's a no-children-kind-of-place. A peace-and-quiet-kind-of-place where trouble never visits."

"Sure piece of heaven this is!"
Poppa told her, sniffing the air.

"Who wants to have trouble on holiday anyway?" I said.

"That's what we like to hear," said Poppa, holding Momma's hands and twirling her around. "That's the way, aha-aha, we like it!" Then he turned to us, "Don't worry, girls, in the next few days there'll be lots of folks here."

Flora and I helped carry the stuff into the house. Momma went straight to the kitchen. This was really one end of the living-room.

"You two should be all right in here," said Poppa, helping us to put our things in the smaller bedroom.

After supper we went to bed. As soon as Momma put out the lamp, the noises started up outside. Crickets chirped. Frogs croaked. A monkey howled in the jungle. Then something started to snort right

50

under the window.

"What's that?" whispered Flora, wrapping her arms around my neck.

"A hungry racoon." I said the first thing that came into my head. Flora soon fell asleep. I took her arms away from my neck.

The next morning when we got up, Poppa was leaving. "See you later," he said.

"Where are you going, Poppa?"

"Busman's holiday, remember?"

"Must you go today?" said Flora.

"Afraid so," said Poppa.

"What about the swing?" I said. "You promised."

"And what about the tree-house?" said Flora.

"Girls, girls!" my father said, as if he was steadying wild horses. "I'll work only half a day and be back for lunch. I promise."

"I hate busman's holidays," said Flora. "We'll be bored."

"No you won't. You'll find lots to do, I bet," said Poppa, waving us goodbye. We grumbled after he drove off. But it wasn't long after, we were playing happily in the house. Soon we became too noisy for Momma.

"For heaven's sake, Melanie and Flora!" she said. "Get out from under my feet. You shouldn't be indoors when there's so much to see and do outside." But as soon as we ran out of the door she called out, "Don't you go wandering too far now. Play where you can see the house."

We saw a footpath under the trees and decided to go for a walk. It was so hot the heat did a strange dance on the ground. We gazed up at the trees, huge and still.

"They are giants looking down at us," Flora whispered. But soon we began playing a game with them, walking in and out of their shadows. Then I snapped off a leaf from an almond tree and started fanning myself.

"I am melting like an ice-cream," I said.

"Don't mention that word," said Flora, "I could eat a barrel of the stuff."

"Forget it," I said. "Let's look for fruit instead."

The first fruit trees we saw were slipper mangoes but the fruits were too hard and green. The cashews were ripe but we didn't want something that tangy.

"Ooh! Look!" said Flora, pointing to some plum trees. The plums were like golden balls dangling high, high above us. Just then a flock of yellow-head parrots flew overhead, chattering noisily. They dived down on the trees and started to eat the golden plums. As they ate they dropped pieces of the skins and wet yellow bits. Some fell on our heads.

Running away, we shouted back at them, "Greedy, greedy parrots!"

Flora and I kept on running until we reached a stream. The water glistened like glass.

"This must be Bright Springs," I told Flora. Scooping up water in our hands, we drank and washed our faces and watched silvery fishes darting like needles in and out of the mangrove roots. Then we started to hop from stone to stone. I took my shoes off but Flora didn't.

"Take your shoes off, Flora," I said. "It's slippery."

"I don't want to. The moss on the stones will tickle my feet," she said.

I was in the middle of the stream when I

"Take your shoes off, Flora," I said. "It's slippery."

heard SPLAAAAAASSSH! I looked round. In the water I saw Flora's skirt billowing out like a balloon. She was splashing about and screaming. I got hold of her plaits. She screamed louder. I grabbed her skirt and fished her out.

"Look at my clothes! I'm soaked," she cried.

"It's your fault. You slipped because you had your shoes on," I told her.

Flora flapped about. She opened and shut her little mouth like a fish. She tried to wring the water out of her plaits.

"Do something!" she cried, looking as if she had swallowed the whole stream.

"Don't be a baby," I said. "The sun is hot as fire. Your clothes will soon dry." I helped her to take them off and spread them on the grass. Then I lent her my shorts.

"I'm hungry," said Flora after a while.

"There are guavas over there. Let's get some," I said, running off to a clump of trees at the edge of the clearing.

We chose the easiest tree to climb and soon we were standing in the crook of two strong branches. Guavas were hanging down all around us, dangling in our faces and sitting on our heads. We couldn't move without elbowing them and knocking them to the ground. The smell almost knocked us over too. We made sure to hang on good as we picked the ripest. They were lemony-yellow outside with tiny pink seeds inside.

"I didn't know guavas could taste so nice," said Flora. "But even guavas aren't as nice as sweets."

"Fruits are friendly. Sweets are rotters. Remember that and keep your choppers," I said.

"You sound just like Grandma," said Flora, and we laughed until tears came to our eyes. Then Flora said, "It's not fair, we should be crocodiles, then we could eat anything without worrying. Poppa says crocodiles just keep on growing new teeth every time they need them."

We were so busy chattering, arguing and giggling that we forgot where we were. We forgot the time. Flora even forgot her clothes drying by the stream. All of a sudden we heard rustlings below us. The bushes changed shape and started to move.

"Eeeeeek! It's a crocodile!" said Flora.

"That's silly. You won't find crocodiles round here," I said. "They like to be on the riverbanks and in the swamps."

Suddenly a loud MOOOOO! echoed through the trees. Flora screamed and hugged me tightly. A black bull charged out of the jungle and headed straight towards us. It had the longest, sharpest horns.

Scruuuuunch! Splaaaat! we heard a few seconds later.

"He's eating guavas right under our tree," I whispered.

"We can't get down," Flora whispered. "I'm scared."

"He'll go away when he's had enough," I said.

"Suppose he doesn't?" asked Flora, starting to throw half-green guavas at him.

"Don't do that! He'll stay even longer," I said. The bull mooed again. Soon some cows came along.

"See! His whole family is here," I cried. "We'll never get down now."

Then the sun went in.

"Ooh!" said Flora, "it's getting dark."

"Don't be silly. The sun's just behind a

cloud," I said. The bull mooed again and the cows mooed back. Flora screamed. I looked through the trees. I couldn't see our house. Everything was quiet except for the noisy chewing below us.

"Dinner must be ready and Momma will be looking for us," said Flora.

"Yes," I said. "Let's shout for her."

When that didn't work we screamed and screamed. It felt like we'd been there for hours. At last we heard voices. Poppa and Momma were looking for us. At first we couldn't see them but they kept calling out, "Melanie! Flora! Where are you?"

The cows started up their mooing again.

"Over here! In the guava tree," we tried to shout above the noise.

Then at last we saw Poppa. He was running ahead. He saw us too and shooed the cows away. Then Momma came and

"Over here! In the guava tree," we tried to shout above the noise.

they both helped us down from the tree.

"Where are your clothes, Flora?" asked Momma.

"They're drying," sobbed Flora.

"You see what happens when you don't listen?" said Momma. "Never stray from the house again, you hear? You gave us the fright of our lives."

Flora kept right on sobbing. Poppa and Momma said they were happy we were safe, but they told us off all the way home.

"And I hope you haven't stuffed yourselves with guavas because your dinner is long ready," said Momma when we got in the house.

During dinner we hardly said a word. But afterwards our parents wanted to know exactly how we had ended up in a tree.

"Never ever go near that stream again," said Momma when we had finished.

Then Poppa said, "I had hoped we'd left trouble behind us. But it seems I was expecting too much. Now, I'll ask you girls one question and after that we'll say no more about the matter. What kind of holiday do you think Momma and I will have if you continue to cause so much trouble?"

I waited for Flora to say something. But she was too comfortable in Momma's lap. Anyway, Poppa was looking hard at me.

"A busman's holiday?" I said in a thin voice.

When I'm nervous I always seem to say the first thing that pops into my head. My parents' eyes flashed at each other and then they burst out laughing. Soon Flora and I were laughing too.

*Mr Williams left us to talk among ourselves
for a few minutes.*

There's More to a Banana

"This term I want you to do a project on tropical fruits," Mr Williams announced to the class when we came back from holiday.

"Great!" we cried.

"Easy-peasy," said Sammy.

"That may be so, Sam," said Mr Williams. "But don't forget that presentation is important. I want your best writing along with your best drawings, photos and anything else you can think of."

Mr Williams left us to talk among ourselves for a few minutes.

"I'll do one of the citrus fruits," said my friend Elena.

"That's a whole lot of fruits to choose from," I said.

"Well, I don't like lemons and limes." Elena made an awful face. "So that only leaves oranges and grapefruits, right?"

"I'll do guavas," said Jenny Silvers, who sat behind me. She had a voice which squeaked in your ears.

"Guavas!" cried Sammy. "They're cow food and they have a pongy smell."

"Don't be silly," said Jenny. "Next you'll be telling me that cows eat guava jelly." Cries of *yum-yum* rippled through the class.

"I'll do mangoes," said David Young. "Because I know a lot about them."

"No! I want to do mangoes," I cried.

"I said it first, so there!" said David.

Several other people began to shout that they wanted to do mangoes. I shook my head and put my hands over my ears. Then

66

Joel, who'd chosen mangoes too, decided to switch to breadfruit.

"That's not a fruit. Whoever heard of a fruit you have to boil, fry or bake before you can eat it? It's more like bread plus fruit," said Sammy grinning wildly. "Get it?"

Everybody started to laugh. Mr Williams cleared his throat. The class went quiet.

"Enough!" he said sharply. "I see I shall have to help you to choose your fruits. But not now. Let's get on with the next lesson first."

We settled down and forgot about the project until hometime. On our way out, Mr Williams asked each of us to pick a piece of paper from a tin on his table. Each piece of paper had the name of a fruit written on it.

"Bananas!" I read when I unfolded mine. "Of all the fruits in the world I had to get bananas!" Suddenly the project didn't seem like such a good idea after all.

"It's not fair," I said when I met up with Flora outside.

"What's wrong?" Flora asked.

"A rotten project on rotten bananas," I said. "That's what's wrong."

"Why? I don't understand," said Flora.

"I wanted to do mangoes. I had the whole thing planned," I said. "But David Young got mangoes and I picked the paper with bananas on it."

"Swap with David then," said Flora.

"He won't. He's real mean and a creep," I said. "What do I know about bananas anyway?"

"I guess as much as you know about mangoes," said Flora. "Just because you've got seventy-three mango seeds in your collection, doesn't mean you know more about mangoes than bananas. Besides, you like bananas a lot, right?"

"Not any more, I don't," I said.

"Since when?" Flora asked.

"Since I've got to do a project on them."

"I'll tell you what," said Flora. "Why don't you draw pictures of all kinds of bananas and fill up your book with them: green and ripe, big and small, jungle bananas and even whole bunches?"

"Oh yes! And what shall I write about the pictures?" I said.

"Plenty," went on Flora. "Under a baby banana you can write 'Don't eat me until I grow up'. And under a jungle banana … 'I'm wild'."

"Very funny," I said. "You don't know how to be helpful, that's your problem."

"Yes I do," said Flora. "But only when you

really, really need it."

I glared at her.

We arrived home, still arguing. My father took one look at me and said jokingly, "Oh, Grandma! What a long face you've got today!"

"As long as a banana," Flora said, laughing at her own joke.

"Shut up," I hissed.

"Shush!" said my father. "What's the problem?"

"BANANAS!" I groaned, and I explained about the project.

"Sooooooooo," he said. "Where's the problem?"

"The problem is I really, really wanted to do mangoes."

"Sometimes we have to do things we don't like. That's a fact of life," said my father.

"What's the problem?"

"And another fact is, when working on a project you must always start with what you know. Read up on what you don't know or ask those who do."

"Like me," said Flora.

"You! What can *you* tell me?" I said.

"Lots. The banana is a very soft, fleshy fruit, but it doesn't have lashings of juice like mangoes and oranges. When it's ripe even a baby can peel it, but when it's green you need a knife to get the skin off. You can't eat a green banana unless you cook it first. You can make banana chips, dumplings and flour. The banana is a longish fruit, as long as…"

"Stop, Flora!" my father said, laughing.

I said nothing. I couldn't believe Flora knew so much about bananas.

All that weekend I worried and fussed about

my project. I told everyone who came to the house about it, and everyone had something to say.

My Uncle Bill sang, "Yes, we have no bananas. We have no bananas today."

"Look at me. I'm as fit as a flea," said my grandmother twirling round. "That's because I'm a banana-a-day person. I eat them raw. I eat them cooked. But the best dish for me is salted mackerel with boiled green bananas. Believe me child, there's more to that fruit than meets the eye."

On Sunday I wrote down everything I had learnt. Then I added a little more each day.

The next Friday afternoon the class read out their first reports. David talked on and on about mangoes. I could have bopped him. Elena had so much to say about oranges that Mr Williams told her to leave some of it for next week. Gary Meddows knew a lot of interesting facts about watermelons, but nobody was surprised. His father grew them in his back garden. It was covered in miles of tangled watermelon vines. They ran along the ground like crazy, turning corners and twisting themselves around anything that got in their way. When Gary finished reading, the whole class clapped. Next Sisty read her report on the sapodilla.

"Very interesting, Sisty," said Mr Williams looking at his watch. "We have time for one more. Melanie, shall we have bananas today?"

I looked at my book. I sighed. Part of the fun of doing a project is seeing who can find the most exciting title. Elena had "Oranges Are Best". David Young's was "A Bucketful of Mangoes", while Sisty called hers "Gummy-gummy Sapodillas". I only had one word. In a very thin voice I read out "Bananas". Everybody sniggered. I pretended I didn't care and read on. "The banana is a longish fruit and some are curved and look like tiny boomerangs. When ripe the banana is yellow, soft and fleshy, but it doesn't have lashings of juice like oranges and mangoes. And even a baby can peel the skin off. But oh boy! When it's green the skin is stuck on so hard you have to use a knife to cut it away. You can boil green bananas or make chips or dumplings from them, and even flour for porridge—"

"What about bananas with brown spots on them?" cried somebody.

"I call those Dalmatian bananas," said Sammy, grinning. "Get it?"

"Not funny," said Jenny Silvers in her squeaky voice. And everybody started to giggle.

75

"Carry on, Melanie," said Mr Williams.

"Bananas grow in hot countries like the West Indies, Ecuador, Mexico, Belize, Australia, the Philippines and hundreds of other places. They like a hot climate but if the weather gets too hot the leaves of the plant shrivel up. My grandma says that there's more to a banana than meets the eye, but I don't know what she means."

"Good, Melanie," said Mr Williams. "I won't spoil it by explaining what your gran means. You'll find out for yourself soon enough."

That evening my father said, "Reading something interesting, Mel?"

"Not really," I said. "It's a book on bananas I got from Mr Williams."

"Have you learnt anything new?" he asked, looking over my shoulder.

"Yes," I said. "You didn't tell me that bananas have names. It says so in this book."

"Sometimes it's more fun to find out things for yourself," my father said. "The names are beautiful, don't you think? Robusta, Lacatan, Gros Michel, Giant Cavendish, Dwarf Cavendish, Valery. And there's the Mons Mari species in Australia. Anyway, how did you get on at school today?"

"All right, I suppose," I said glumly.

"We've got a little surprise to cheer you up," said my father. "I've arranged for us to visit my friend's banana plantation next weekend."

I felt better already. I couldn't help giving him a tiny smile. My father smiled back. "That's more like it," he said.

Early Saturday morning we drove to

Manuel's banana plantation. We got out of the pick-up truck and a huge, noisy grey dog bounded towards us. Flora and I tucked ourselves between Poppa and Momma. My father patted the dog and she stopped barking and started to wag her tail.

"My friends," cried Manuel from the verandah, "you've made it, I see."

"Wouldn't have missed it for the world," said my father. Then Manuel looked down at Flora and me. He grinned. I saw his gold tooth glistening in the sunlight.

"Which of you girls would like to be a banana expert, then?" he asked.

"Me," I said. "I've got to do a project."

"Yes," said Flora, "and she wants you to tell her lots and lots so she can get good marks."

"I'll do my best," smiled Manuel.

The farm door opened in a hurry. Manuel's wife, Theresa, came rushing out

*My father patted the dog and she stopped barking
and started to wag her tail.*

on to the verandah.

"*Hola mis amigos,*" she cried, shaking my father's hand. Then she and my mother wrapped their arms around each other, talking all the while. Theresa spoke Spanish and a little English. My mother spoke English dotted with a Spanish word here and there. It sounded funny but they seemed to understand each other very well.

A few minutes later Theresa turned to us.

"*Hola* Melanie and Flora," she said. "Something to drink, yes?"

Before we could answer she had disappeared into the house, and soon we were holding a glass in one hand and a slice of cake in the other.

"Banana and cinnamon, mmmmmm!" I said, sipping the frothy drink.

"Can I have your cake, Mel?" teased Flora. "You don't like bananas any more, remember?"

"This is different," I said, gulping down my drink to the last drop and biting into the cake, which was delicious. Manuel stood up. He slapped a black hat on his head and eased the strap under his chin.

"Let's go," he said, walking down the steps. My father, Flora and I followed him. My mother stayed with Theresa. They told us they had a lot of catching up to do.

The plantation was right behind the farmhouse. Everywhere we looked were rows and rows and rows of banana plants.

"Owee!" squealed Flora. "They're like an army of soldiers standing still."

My father and Manuel laughed. The plants grew in orderly straight lines with equal space between them. Every plant had one bunch of very green bananas hanging on it. The banana leaves were broad and long. They were like green umbrellas shading the bananas from the hot sun. We walked between the rows of plants where it was shady and cool.

"Look, I'm nearly as tall as this tree," said Flora, standing under a huge bunch of bananas.

"It's not a tree, it's a plant," corrected Manuel.

"When is a tree not a tree?" my father shouted. He had stopped to take pictures and was coming to join us again, adjusting his camera strap over his shoulder.

"When I can't climb it," Flora shouted back.

Manuel laughed. "Very clever."

"When the lumberjack cries TIMBER!" said my father.

"You read too many comics my friend,"

"Look, I'm nearly as tall as this tree," said Flora.

said Manuel. "What do you think, Melanie?"

"When it's a plant," I said.

"Very witty, but in order to get full marks, tell me what you notice about this," said Manuel, pointing at a stem.

"It's much softer than the trunk of a tree," said Flora, wrapping her arms around it.

"And there's no bark and no woody part," I said. "And no lumberjack would want to chop it down because there's no timber, right?"

"Go to the top of the class," said my father.

What a lot I'm learning already! I thought to myself as I sat on a stump and wrote up my notes.

"Now," said Manuel, "how about a little maths?"

"What's maths got to do with bananas?" I asked.

"Plenty," said Manuel. "I'm nearly two metres tall. Can you guess how big this plant is?"

"Three metres," shouted Flora.

"Taller," I said.

"Good," said Manuel. "This plant is five metres, but I've some that are shorter too. Now take a plant each and count the number of leaves."

My father had to help Flora because the leaves kept swaying about in the breeze. I counted seventy. Flora and my father counted sixty on theirs.

"Good," said Manuel, "there are sixty to seventy leaves on each plant. And I'll tell you something else: each week a banana plant grows one leaf."

"Really? So it took seventy weeks to grow all the leaves on my plant," I said.

"Great guns! That was quick," said Manuel.

"I'm quick at counting too," said Flora.

"Of course you are," said my father.

Manuel pulled back the leaves from a bunch of bananas. "Do you notice anything strange about how the bunch hangs?"

My father bent down, his hands almost touching the ground. I knew he was giving us a clue.

"The bunch grows downwards on the plant," I cried.

"Correct," said Manuel. "And what about the bananas?"

"They grow upwards."

"That's funny," said Flora, "the bunch grows downwards and the bananas grow upwards."

Then Manuel told us to count the number of bananas on a hand. A hand is really another name for a cluster of bananas. We counted fifteen. Manuel told us that a good bunch always has eight or nine hands.

"If bananas have hands then hands should have fingers, right?" said Flora, trying to be funny.

"Actually, a single banana *is* called a finger," said Manuel.

"See! I'm right!" Flora grinned.

"I think it's time for a little diversion," said Manuel, winking at my father. "Ready, girls?" We nodded. We walked to a clearing where the earth was dry and the grass grew in tufts. Manuel kept looking at the ground, searching for something with his foot. Suddenly he pulled up a handful of grass. We saw a hole so small even Flora's fist couldn't fit in it. Manuel tapped around it with his feet. My father joined him. Flora and I stood well back. Watching them reminded me of the Mexican hat dance, where dancers circle round a hat with their hands behind their backs.

"There it is!" cried Manuel suddenly. "Isn't she a beauty?"

Flora and I stared at the black, velvety, hairy tarantula. It came a little way out of the hole. I jumped back. Flora screamed and the tarantula scarpered back into the hole.

"Tarantulas aren't interested in us," said Manuel. "They much prefer to hide in a bunch of bananas and travel to foreign countries free of charge."

We all laughed except Flora. She ran off.

The other end of the plantation was busy and noisy. Some workers were chopping down bunches of bananas with sharp machetes. Others were loading up trucks and shouting orders at each other.

"There are only green bananas here," I

*Flora screamed and the tarantula scarpered
back into the hole.*

said. "Why is that?"

"We only send green bananas abroad," said Manuel. "Ripe bananas would be spoilt by the end of their journey."

"Phew!" I said. "What a lot there is to know about bananas! My book is nearly full."

On our way back to the house a truck with "Cavendish" written on the side roared past us.

"Ah! Cavendish," I said. "Do you grow Robusta, Lacatan and Gros Michel too?"

"She is a little expert on the quiet," Manuel told my father. My father gave me a huge smile.

"I'll never ever forget today, Manuel," I said. "Thank you very much."

I spent most of Sunday designing my book. It was in the shape of a huge banana. The front cover was crayoned in yellow and the back in green. On each page I wrote the name of a species of banana. Afterwards I drew some pictures and cut out others from a *National Geographic* magazine to make a collage of a plantation. I had so much to write, it took the whole week to finish it.

"Don't forget to leave enough space for my wonderful photos," smiled my father.

Two weeks later Mr Williams asked us to show our projects to the class. Soon everybody was busy piling the display tables with fruits, leaves, seeds, pictures and posters. There were cakes, sweets and fruit preserves.

"It's like harvest time," said Sammy, and everyone agreed.

Each day five people read out their projects and it took a week before everyone had had a turn. I was hoping mine would be the best, but everyone else had worked very hard too. My turn came on the last day.

"I shall leave the title to the end," I told the class.

Then I held up my book to show them the front and back covers.

"Brilliant!" they cried.

I didn't need to read out my work because I remembered most of what I had written. I just showed the pictures and talked as I turned the pages.

At the end I said, "Although I have learnt so much about the banana, there is a whole lot more I don't know. And that's why I have called my project 'There's More to a Banana Than Meets the Eye'."

"Well done, Melanie," said Mr Williams. "In fact I have never seen the whole class work so hard on a project before."

"Well sir," said Sammy, "you could say there is more to *us* than meets the eye, right?"

And the whole class laughed, even Mr Williams.

THE

END